The American

1764 KAYA, an adventurous Nez Perce girl whose deep love for horses and respect for nature nourish her spirit

1774 FELICITY, a spunky, spritely colonial girl, full of energy and independence

1824 JOSEFINA, a Hispanic girl whose heart and hopes are as big as the New Mexico sky

1854 KIRSTEN, a pioneer girl of strength and spirit who settles on the frontier

1864 ADDY, a courageous girl determined to be free in the midst of the Civil War

1904 SAMANTHA, a bright Victorian beauty, an orphan raised by her wealthy grandmother

1934 KIT, a clever, resourceful girl facing the Great Depression with spirit and determination

1944 MOLLY, who schemes and dreams on the home front during World War Two

1974 JULIE, a fun-loving girl from San Francisco who faces big changes—and creates a few of her own

1976

GOOD LUCK, *Ivy*

By LISA YEE

ILLUSTRATIONS ROBERT HUNT

VIGNETTES NIKA KORNIYENKO, SUSAN McALILEY

★ American Girl®

Questions or comments? Call 1-800-845-0005, visit **americangirl.com**,
or write to Customer Service, American Girl, 8400 Fairway Place,
Middleton, WI 53562-0497.

Printed in China
07 08 09 10 11 12 LEO 10 9 8 7 6 5 4 3 2 1

PICTURE CREDITS
The following individuals and organizations have generously
given permission to reprint images contained in "Looking Back":
p. 17, p. 55—BRUCE LEE and the Bruce Lee likeness are trademarks and copyrights
of Concord Moon LP. All rights reserved; p. 73—courtesy Lisa Yee; pp. 74–75—courtesy
Lisa Yee and Marylin Yee (Marylin Yee family); North Wind Picture Archive (Canton, China);
Library of Congress (mining camp); © Corbis (railroad); pp. 76–77—Library of Congress
(Chinatown art, washer ad, earthquake photos); California Historical Society (immigrants);
pp. 78–79—© Charles E. Rotkin/Corbis (Chinatown, NY); © Doug Pensinger/Getty Images
Sport (Michelle Kwan); © Bettmann/Corbis (Maya Lin); © Frank Capri/Getty Images
(Amy Tan); BRUCE LEE and the Bruce Lee likeness are trademarks and copyrights of
Concord Moon LP. All rights reserved; courtesy Lisa Yee (Yee family).
Author photo on cover by Mieke Kramer.

Cataloging-in-Publication Data available from Library of Congress

Special thanks to Coach Parrisa Peik of the
South Pasadena Payke Gymnastics Academy.
With gratitude to Judy Yung, Ph.D., and to K. L. Kiu.

TO JULIE UEHARA
AND DEBBIE LOESCHER
FOR YOUR FRIENDSHIP
AND KINDNESS

TABLE OF CONTENTS

GOOD LUCK, IVY

CHAPTER ONE
OFF BALANCE   1

CHAPTER TWO
A NEW TWIST   16

CHAPTER THREE
IVY'S DILEMMA   33

CHAPTER FOUR
DRAGONS RULE   49

CHAPTER FIVE
THE BIG DAY   58

LOOKING BACK   73

A SNEAK PEEK AT *MEET JULIE*   81

Ivy's Family

Mr. Ling
*Ivy's father, who
expects his children to
do their very best*

Mrs. Ling
*Ivy's mother, who is
going to law school*

Ivy
*A ten-year-old girl who
loves gymnastics and wants
to make her family proud*

Andrew
*Ivy's twelve-year-old
brother, who studies
kung fu*

Missy
*Ivy's little sister, who
is three years old*

GUNG GUNG
*Ivy's grandfather, who owns
a Chinese restaurant*

PO PO
*Ivy's gentle grandmother,
who can see into Ivy's heart*

JULIE
*Ivy's best friend, who
gets together with Ivy
on the weekends*

OFF BALANCE

 Ivy Ling looked around the dining table and let out a sigh. "Chinese food again? Why can't we have American food like everyone else, and eat hamburgers or spaghetti?"

"First of all, spaghetti is Italian," said her brother, Andrew, slipping into his know-it-all voice. "And second, many believe that Marco Polo brought noodles to Italy from China—so that would make it Chinese, too!"

Ivy rolled her eyes. It wasn't that she disliked Chinese food. It was just that she didn't like eating it every single day. It seemed as if her mom never had time to cook anymore, so instead she served takeout

1

from Ivy's grandparents' restaurant, the Happy Panda.

Ivy poked at her tofu with her chopsticks and watched it wiggle. It was far more interesting than Andrew, who was now discussing his favorite subject—himself.

"Master Jung says I'm doing great. Bruce Lee was thirteen when he started taking kung fu. That's a year older than I am, and he was the best martial artist in the entire world."

It was impossible living with Andrew. For example, take last weekend, when Julie Albright was visiting. *The Brady Bunch* had just started, and he strolled right in and changed the channel!

"Hey," Ivy had yelled.

"Sorry," Andrew said, not looking sorry at all. "But *The Six Million Dollar Man* is on."

"We were here first," Ivy protested.

Andrew moved his kung fu trophies to the front of the fireplace mantel, sliding Ivy's gymnastics trophies toward the back. "You have to do what I tell you," he replied smugly. "In China, the eldest son is treated like royalty."

"Andrew," Ivy retorted, getting up and turning

the channel back to *The Brady Bunch*, "I'm not sure if you noticed, but we're in America."

Both girls giggled as Andrew stormed off.

Ivy smiled, remembering the incident. "May I call Julie?" she asked, looking up from her plate.

"After dinner," her mother said.

"*And,*" her father added, "after your homework."

Ivy and Julie were best friends. Julie used to live right across the street, until last September when her parents got divorced. Then Julie moved away with her mother and sister, leaving Ivy all alone. At least that was how it felt. Sure, they talked on the phone, and on the weekends Julie often stayed with her father, who still lived across the street. But it wasn't the same as having your best friend right there—going to school together, practicing gymnastics together, and playing together almost every day as Ivy and Julie had done since kindergarten.

If I were at Julie's house, Ivy mused, *we'd be eating something normal like tuna casserole or meat loaf—and we could watch television without any annoying brothers trying to take over.* Plus, Julie's dad had a color TV, while the Lings just had their old black-and-white set. Ivy sighed. Even Great-Uncle Henry had a color television, which he'd won on *The Price Is Right* game show. And that hardly seemed fair, because Great-Uncle Henry was color-blind.

"How was school today?" Mr. Ling asked, shaking Ivy out of her thoughts.

"Good," Ivy said. "Mr. Nader says that we'll be going on a field trip to the Exploratorium."

"We finger painted," Missy volunteered, proudly pointing to a splatter of blue on her red shirt.

"I aced my history test," Andrew answered.

Everyone turned to Mrs. Ling. "I'm afraid I'm behind on my homework," she admitted. "Plus I have a huge exam coming up."

"You'll do great, Mama," Ivy assured her.

"Thanks, honey."

It was sort of strange having a mother who was in school. Last year, Mrs. Ling had quit her job and enrolled at Hastings Law School. Even though her trim figure, feathered hair, and stylish wraparound dresses made her look young, Ivy's mother was the oldest student in her class.

At first Ivy thought it was exciting. Every day her mom would come home with stories about her stern professors, and everyone would laugh. But after a while she didn't tell as many funny stories. Then, when Ivy's father got a second job, it seemed as if Ivy hardly ever saw her parents. And when she did, her mother was either rushing around or studying, and her father was always tired.

Why do things have to change? Ivy wondered. Why couldn't everything just stay the way it was when her mother wasn't in law school, and her father didn't have to work two jobs, and her best friend lived right across the street?

Mr. Ling put on his jacket to head to his night job. Ivy thought he looked handsome in his security guard uniform. "Don't forget your homework, Ivy!" he told her.

Ivy flipped open her denim binder. Even though she had been assigned the book report a week ago, she hadn't gotten very far. Just as she was nearing the end, her mother asked, "Ivy, would you mind giving Missy her bath tonight?"

"But I was going to call Julie."

"You can call her tomorrow."

"But Mama, I really need to talk to Julie—"

"Tomorrow, Ivy."

Ivy tipped the box of Mr. Bubble into the clawfoot tub and watched the bubbles build. She tested the water to make sure it wasn't too hot.

"That looks like a lovely bath," Mrs. Ling said as she came in and handed Ivy some clean towels.

"Mama, will you be in law school forever?"

"Oh, honey, it's just a couple more years. I know it's been hard on the family, and you kids have been a big help. This morning Missy even fed Jasmine and Wonton their cat food." Mrs. Ling bit her lip. "Ivy, law school is something I've wanted to do for a long time. I'm studying extra hard to make all of you proud of me when I become a lawyer."

The bathroom was getting steamy. Ivy turned off the hot water. "I'm already proud of you, Mama."

Mrs. Ling kissed her daughter on the top of her head. "Thank you, Ivy."

Ivy wished her mother would stay. She missed the long talks they used to have before her mom became so busy.

"Are the bubbles ready?" Missy hollered.

"Come on in," Ivy shouted back.

After Missy was scrubbed clean and in her pajamas, Ivy marched her into their bedroom. On

Missy's side, pictures of baby animals lined the walls. Ivy's wall was plastered with posters of Olga Korbut and other gymnasts, and resting on her bed was a pillow with an ivy leaf pattern that Julie had made for her. Behind the door hung a Chinese dress of shimmering red silk. Ivy thought the dress was too beautiful to be kept hidden in the closet. "It's red for good luck," Mrs. Ling had said when she gave it to Ivy last January at Chinese New Year. It was hard to believe that was five whole months ago. Ivy hoped the dress would still fit her the next time she wore it!

As Ivy picked up the toys scattered around the room, Mrs. Ling said good night to Missy and tucked her into bed. Before the lights were even out, Missy's eyes were closed. Ivy smiled at her little sister, who looked like an angel with her short black hair framing her chubby face. She was snuggling Roary, her beat-up little lion. It was hard to believe that this was the same mischievous girl Ivy had to chase around the house.

Slowly, so as not to wake her, Ivy opened the curtains. She flipped the light switch on and off a

couple of times and then waited. And waited. Last
year, the lights in Julie's old room across the way
would have flickered back. But tonight, there was
only darkness.

"She's not there," a small voice said.

Ivy whipped around. "Missy, I thought you were
asleep!"

"Nope," she said. "Julie's not there."

"I know that," Ivy said sharply. She was glad the
room was dark and her sister couldn't see her
turning red. "Go to sleep, Missy."

For Ivy, the best time of the day was when school
got out. Every afternoon, she would hurry to the
Chinatown YWCA to practice with the rest of the
Twisters gymnastics team.

"Girls, please gather around!" Coach Gloria
was young and pretty. Her thick brown hair
was tied in a ponytail, and she wore several
rubber bands on her wrist in case anyone
forgot hers. "Win or lose, after this year's all-
city competition, we're having a big party!"

"Ooooh! Can we have pizza?" Susie asked.

"Well, that's up to all of you. We're going to need a fund-raiser for our party. Any suggestions?"

"A lemonade stand?" said Cindy.

"Or a car wash?" said Karen.

"What about a bake sale?" Jennifer suggested.

Everyone began talking at once, and soon it was decided. The Twisters gymnastics team bake sale would take place that weekend.

Ivy's hand shot up in the air. "I'll bring my mom's famous Chinese almond cookies!" Soon everyone was volunteering brownies and cupcakes and other treats.

"This all sounds great," Coach Gloria said. "But now it's time for practice. The all-city tournament is coming up fast."

Ivy pulled her black hair into a short ponytail and then did her stretches before taking her position on the mat. As always, the minute Ivy heard the music, she relaxed and began her floor exercise routine. Her body loved doing the flips and twists and turns. Her mother always said that even when she was a baby, she was tumbling all over the living room.

"Your floor work's looking good, Ivy," Coach

Gloria noted. "Are you ready to get on the beam?"

Ivy gulped. Her coach expected the girls to master the floor exercise, the vault, the uneven bars, and the balance beam. In the past, Ivy had done well in the all-around competition. That is, until the tournament before last. No matter how hard she tried to shake the incident out of her mind, she couldn't.

Ivy had just mounted the balance beam, smiling confidently. As she went through her mandatory movements—split jump, pivot, tuck jump—her body moved exactly as it was supposed to. Then, as she began a back walkover, she felt herself wobble. Panic shot through her as she struggled to regain her balance. But it was too late. Ivy could hear the crowd gasp as she hit the cushioned mat with a thud.

Her shoulder hurt and her legs were shaking as she got up. *Ten seconds, ten seconds.* Ivy knew she had only ten seconds to get back on the beam or risk more point deductions. Her hands were sweaty and her arms felt weak. She tried to get back on the beam, but slipped and fell again. Then the tears began. She couldn't turn them off. Mortified, she ran away and hid in the girls' bathroom, unable to face the judges, the audience, or her team.

Ivy had just mounted the balance beam, smiling confidently.

Trying to push the memory out of her mind, Ivy slowly approached the balance beam. The beam was sixteen feet long, four inches wide, and four feet off the ground. It seemed miles high.

"Are you still feeling unsure of yourself?" Coach Gloria asked.

Ivy bit her lip. "A little."

"Try to set your fears aside, and give it your best shot."

Ivy took a deep breath and lifted herself onto the beam.

"Okay, let's go, Ivy!" she heard her coach saying.

"Flat foot, lift your back leg higher!

"Ivy, you lost your line. Don't drop that leg!

"Plié, jump straight up. Again—higher!"

I can't do anything right, Ivy scolded herself. With each move she felt as if she was losing control. Ivy couldn't look at her coach.

"Okay, let's take a break," Coach Gloria finally said.

Ivy exhaled and jumped off the beam.

"You know that Olga Korbut won an Olympic gold medal in balance beam," said Coach Gloria.

"And gold in floor, too," added Ivy.

Coach Gloria smiled. "She helped her team win gold as well. She's why you're here, right?"

Ivy nodded. She could still recall her family crowded around the TV set four years ago, watching the petite Russian gymnast compete in the Olympics. Even though Ivy had been only six years old at the time, she was mesmerized. At that moment she dreamed of becoming a gymnast like Olga Korbut. Later that fall, Ivy started lessons.

Olga Korbut

"Olga can do backward aerial somersaults with her eyes closed," Ivy mumbled. "I can't even stay on the balance beam."

"When she introduced that move at the Munich Olympics," her coach began, "it might have been the first time the world saw it, but it wasn't the first time Olga had tried it. She practiced and practiced and practiced to make it look so easy." Coach Gloria looked into Ivy's eyes. "You have a natural talent, Ivy. All you need to do is push past your fear."

Practice, practice, practice, Ivy said to herself. *Practice, practice, practice.*

Ivy took her time walking to the drinking fountain. Everywhere she looked, she saw her team-mates practicing. On the padded blue mats at the center of the floor, Jennifer and Karen worked on their aerial cartwheels. Off to one side, Susie whirled around the uneven bars. At the far end of the gym, several girls took turns practicing their handsprings off the vault.

Ivy got a drink of water and then returned to the beam area. Some beams were set low to the floor, for beginners. Ivy headed to the regulation-sized beams—the tall ones. *Practice, practice, practice,* she told herself.

Just as Ivy was getting good at her back walk-over, she heard a familiar voice. "Look, there's Ivy!" *Missy!* Ivy pivoted around—and lost her balance. As she hit the mat, Missy screamed, "Mommy, Ivy fell again!"

Ivy jumped up. "I'm okay, Missy," she growled.

"Time to go, Ivy," her mother said.

"Time to go, Ivy!" Missy echoed.

"But Mama, I need to practice. Ten more minutes?"

Her mother looked tired. "Ivy, please. I'm running late and we still have to pick up dinner."

Just my luck, Ivy thought. *Right when I'm getting better, I have to leave.*

"Mrs. Ling," said Coach Gloria, sprinting over. "Thank you! Ivy's volunteered to bring your famous almond cookies to our bake sale this weekend."

"Oh!" Ivy's mother said, looking surprised. "Well, I suppose I can find the time . . ." She glanced at Ivy, who held up crossed fingers. "Yes, I can make those cookies." Mrs. Ling gave her daughter a weary smile.

Coach Gloria turned to Ivy. "You're going to master the balance beam again. Don't worry. You'll do great at the tournament!"

Ivy tried to grin but it felt more like a grimace. She wished she could share her coach's confidence.

"Look at Roary!" Missy called. Mrs. Ling and Coach Gloria laughed. The little stuffed lion was perched on the balance beam.

Great, thought Ivy. *Roary can stay on the beam, so why can't I?*

CHAPTER
TWO
___
A NEW TWIST

On Saturday Ivy awoke to her bed shaking.

Earthquake! Her eyes flashed open. But it wasn't an earthquake. Ivy buried herself under the blankets. "Missy, stop that!"

Her little sister kept jumping on the bed. "Mommy says you have to get up *now* and get ready for Chinese school!"

Ivy grumbled as she rolled out of bed and began to dress. None of her friends had to go to school on Saturday. Why did she?

"It's simple," Andrew explained as he and Ivy walked toward Chinatown. "They want us to suffer."

"But what's the point of it?" protested Ivy. "It's not like we're ever going to use this stuff we're forced to learn."

"True," Andrew agreed. "I'd rather be practicing my kung fu instead of listening to Mrs. Chan ramble on and on."

"And I'd rather be at gymnastics." To prove her point, Ivy did a series of handsprings and cartwheels as they cut through Washington Square Park.

Even though it was early, Chinatown was bustling. Men set up chessboards in Portsmouth Square. Parents hurried their children along as they went about their errands. The delicious smell of roast duck mingled with the scent of incense and fresh herbs. Shopkeepers readied their wares, setting out hand-painted lacquer cabinets and colorful paper fans.

Ivy and Andrew passed the Lucky Five and Dime, where nothing was a nickel or a dime. This sort of bothered Ivy, but Andrew didn't care because one section was crammed with Bruce Lee stuff—posters, T-shirts, mugs, everything. Ivy was glad Julie and Mr. Albright were picking her up after class today. Otherwise,

Bruce Lee

17

she would have to wait forever as her brother
stopped to examine the Bruce Lee merchandise on
their way home.

On the next block, Andrew rapped on the
window of the Happy Panda restaurant. Gung

Gung's face lit up as he hurried
to unlock the door. "Come in!
Come in!"

Ivy's grandparents, Gung Gung
and Po Po, owned the Happy Panda.
It was one of Chinatown's most
popular restaurants. On some nights loyal customers
had to line up to get a table. Ivy's mother often
talked about how her parents had worked long
hours to make the restaurant a success.

Usually the Happy Panda was filled with the
clangor of dishes and the aroma of sizzling garlic
and ginger. Ivy loved the ornate screens and carvings
that decorated the walls, but she knew it was the
food that attracted the crowds. Sometimes strangers
would lean over toward the next table and ask,
"What is that you ordered? It looks delicious!"

But now the restaurant was quiet. Ivy's favorite
times at the Happy Panda were Saturday mornings

before the restaurant opened. That's when she and
Andrew had the Happy Panda—and their grandparents—all to themselves.

"Ivy! Andrew!" Po Po called out. The big tray
she carried with bowls of steaming hot *jook* made her
look even smaller than she was.

Every Saturday before Chinese school, Ivy and
her brother had breakfast with their grandparents.
Ivy stirred her pale rice porridge. Even though jook
wasn't her first choice for breakfast, it was worth it to
spend this special time with Gung Gung and Po Po.

"Come, Ivy," Po Po said, motioning toward the
kitchen. "Bring bowl. Keep me company."

As her grandmother began soaking dried mush-
rooms in big pots of cold water, Ivy sat on her special
stool in the corner of the kitchen. She concentrated
on balancing her bowl of jook on one knee.

"Ivy, eat!" Po Po chided. Ivy smiled. Her grandmother always seemed to know what she was up
to—even with her back turned!

Soon Gung Gung and Andrew joined them.
"He wants more," her grandfather said proudly as
he ladled more jook into Andrew's empty bowl.

"Do you need help around the restaurant?" Ivy

asked hopefully. "I could stay after breakfast."

Gung Gung tried to look stern, but the corners of his eyes crinkled in a smile. "Ivy, you ask that every Saturday. There will be no skipping class!"

"You lucky to go to Chinese school," Po Po chimed in. "School is a privilege some girls in China never have."

"Nice try, Sis," Andrew said with a smirk as they left the Happy Panda and rounded the corner.

Chinese school was in a cramped room above Louie's Number One Bakery. The bulletin boards were covered with posters of the Great Wall of China, scrolls of Chinese characters, and examples of students' work. Andrew's papers were always on display. On occasion, Ivy's were too.

"*Jo sun*," Mrs. Chan said as the twenty students of all ages took their seats. "Good morning."

"Teacher, good morning," they answered back in Chinese. "*Lo see, jo sun.*"

Mrs. Chan reminded Ivy of a hummingbird. Her shiny black hair was pulled back in a tight bun to reveal delicate features, and she was always moving.

"There are almost one billion Chinese in the world," Mrs. Chan lectured the class. "Of those, millions speak in the Cantonese dialect . . ."

Ivy struggled to stay awake as Mrs. Chan droned on. The Chinese language was totally confusing—the same word spoken in a high voice meant something entirely different in a lower voice. Ivy sighed. What difference did it make whether she could speak or read Chinese? This was America. She was American. It seemed like a whole lot of work for nothing.

Then there were all those Chinese characters—more than six thousand of them! Ivy dipped her brush in the dark black ink. There was no way she would master every intricate brush stroke. Even though she was pretty good at Chinese calligraphy, practicing the same strokes and symbols over and over again was so boring. Last week Ivy had finished early, so she painted a monkey alongside her words. That assignment did not make it onto the wall.

After what seemed like hours of repetition, Mrs. Chan turned off the lights and put a transparency of a dragon on the overhead projector. Ivy was happy to close her Chinese vocabulary book. At least this lesson might be interesting. She had a small jade dragon that her grandparents in New York, Ah Yeh and Ah Mah, had brought back from

China when they visited last summer.

"The dragon," Mrs. Chan explained, "is a mythical creature made up of several animals. The body looks like a snake, while the scales and tail resemble a fish. The dragon is a symbol for good luck and one of the most powerful signs in the Chinese zodiac."

Andrew began waving frantically at Mrs. Chan. "Yes, Andrew?"

"Dragons rule! Bruce Lee was born in San Francisco in the year of the dragon," he announced. "His nickname was 'Little Dragon,' and he said that helped bring him good luck. And guess what—I was born in the year of the dragon, too!" Without warning, Andrew assumed a kung fu fighting stance and let out a fierce yell, waking up the boy in front of him.

As the class laughed and Mrs. Chan scowled, Ivy shook her head. Andrew loved being the center of attention. *If he fell off the balance beam in competition, he wouldn't run away,* Ivy thought to herself. *He'd probably take a bow!*

It's just my luck to have a brother like Andrew. Everything comes so easily to him. As if that weren't enough, he was tall for his age, and Ivy could see that his shaggy mop of black hair and cocky grin made the girls swoon. *He's just my dumb brother!* Ivy wanted to shout.

By the time Mrs. Chan had settled the class back down, it was almost time to leave. "Before you go," she said, "I have an extra-credit assignment." Ivy perked up her ears, hoping for an easy way to boost her so-so grade. "It's a family history project," Mrs. Chan explained. "I'd like you to include stories about your relatives. For those of you with siblings in this class, only one of you may work on this. The others can do a biography of a famous Chinese American."

Ivy slumped back in her chair. She needed the extra credit, but this was a hard, complicated assignment. She already had the tournament to worry about, and now this? Maybe she could do the biography instead.

Andrew's hand shot up. "I'll write a report on Bruce Lee!"

"Andrew," Mrs. Chan said, smiling, "you don't need any extra credit, unlike some of the others in here." Ivy's face heated up. She was sure Mrs. Chan was staring at her.

"I'll do it anyway," Andrew declared.

Ivy and several other students groaned.

Mrs. Chan pretended not to hear them. Instead, she said, "Class, good-bye. *Joy geen!*"

"*Lo see, joy geen,*" the students replied. "Teacher, good-bye."

As soon as Ivy cleared the doorway, she ran downstairs.

"Poison Ivy!"

Ivy turned, and there was Julie. "Alley Oop!" Ivy exclaimed, hugging her friend.

Julie linked arms with Ivy. "Come on, my dad's waiting in the car."

"Hi, Ivy, nice to see you!" Mr. Albright said.

"Hi, Mr. Albright," Ivy answered. "Where are we going today?"

"Someplace good," Julie promised. Her straight blond hair was loose around her shoulders. Ivy slid the rubber band off her ponytail.

"Ghirardelli Square!" Ivy announced with delight when the redbrick buildings and big sign came into view.

Mr. Albright dropped the girls

off at the entrance. "See you in one hour," he called.

As Ivy and Julie savored their ice cream cones, they watched the Ghirardelli chocolate churn in huge vats. A heavenly smell wafted through the air. When their ice cream was gone, the two girls lingered in the chocolate shop. There were rows and rows of chocolates, including little chocolate cable cars, thin squares of individually wrapped chocolates, and bags of chocolate drops. But what Ivy loved the most was the wooden barrel filled with broken slabs of chocolate. These were on sale and tasted just as good as—maybe even better than—the fancy chocolates on the shelves.

Ivy dug through the barrel until she found what she was looking for—a big broken chunk of chocolate that cost less than a quarter. She paid for her purchase, and then the girls discussed their next stop as they walked toward Mr. Albright's car.

"Can you let us off at K & B's Groceries?" Julie asked as her father skillfully steered down the twisting turns of Lombard Street. "Ivy needs to pick up some things for her mom."

"Just think of me as your chauffeur," he quipped. "Shall I wait for you?"

"Thanks, but we can walk to my house from there," Ivy said. "It's only a couple of blocks."

K & B's was crowded, but Ivy pushed the cart through the narrow aisles like a pro. Lately she had been helping a lot with the grocery shopping.

"Do you have the list of ingredients?" Julie asked.

"Right here," Ivy said, pulling it out of her denim purse. "My mom says that since the cookies are for the bake sale, we should triple the recipe."

Ivy and Julie left the store, each carrying a brown paper bag. They had felt very grown-up to be grocery shopping on their own. But as they walked up the hill, the bags of flour and sugar grew heavier and heavier. When they reached the tidy yellow townhouse with white trim, both let out sighs of relief.

"We're home!" Ivy called as she and Julie stepped inside.

Andrew was fiddling with the antenna on top of the television as Missy and Roary danced along with the *Sesame Street* Muppets. The volume was turned way down.

"*Shhh*," Andrew said. "Mom's sleeping."

"*Shhh*," said Missy.

Ivy peeked into the dining room. Papers were scattered all over the table. Sure enough, her mother was sleeping with her head down on top of an open book. Ivy and Julie giggled.

"You know," Ivy said as she quietly closed the kitchen door, "we can bake these cookies ourselves. I've seen my mom make them a million times."

"Sure," Julie agreed. "How hard can it be?"

The girls were giddy as Ivy tied her mother's apron around her waist and then set Mrs. Ling's biggest mixing bowl on the counter.

"How many eggs do you think we should use?" asked Julie.

"Well, we want to make a lot of cookies. So I'd say maybe six or seven."

Ivy dumped in half the bag of sugar, and then a little more to be safe. Almond cookies were very sweet! Julie added flour while Ivy stirred. As they plopped the balls of cookie dough onto the baking sheet, Ivy hesitated. "It doesn't look quite the same as when my mom makes them. Oh well."

With the cookies safely in the oven, Ivy and Julie congratulated themselves. Soon, the warm, wonderful smell of cookies baking filled the kitchen.

"Well, we want to make a lot of cookies," said Ivy.

"Wait!" Julie cried. "Ivy, we forgot something."

"What?"

Julie held up a bag of almonds.

"Oh no," Ivy yelped. "They won't be Chinese almond cookies without the almonds! Maybe it's not too late."

Ivy opened the oven—and let out a scream. Almost instantly, the kitchen door flew open. "Ivy, are you all right?" Mrs. Ling shouted. Ivy cringed when she saw her mother's eyes grow big.

The kitchen was a mess. She and Julie were a mess. Worst of all, the cookies were a mess. Mrs. Ling grabbed a hot pad and set the cookie sheet on the stove. Ivy stared at it in horror. The dough had all run together and was puffed up in the center. It was bubbling and steaming like a volcano about to erupt.

"We were just trying to help," Ivy stammered. "I could see that you were tired, and I thought that if we baked the cookies, you could have more time . . ."

Ivy's mother carried the pan to the sink. "I'm touched that you wanted to let me catch up on my rest, but cooking is something you need a grown-up to help you with," Mrs. Ling said. "Why don't we just start all over, and this time I'll bake."

Andrew wandered in and pointed. "What's that supposed to be?"

"Cookies," Ivy mumbled.

"Cookies?" Andrew snorted. "It looks more like a science project! What were you using, the *Twilight Zone* cookbook?" he said as he left the room.

"A cookbook!" Ivy cried. "That's what we need! Mama, what if you gave us your recipe? That way we could bake while you study."

"If we have any questions, we'll ask," Julie promised.

"Well, I do have a lot of work." Mrs. Ling hesitated. "I'll tell you what. I'll study at the kitchen table, so I'll be right here in case you need me."

Soon Ivy's mother was back with her books, and Ivy and Julie were carefully following each step of the recipe.

"This looks a lot better," Ivy said as they rolled the dough into little balls and placed them on the cookie sheet.

"Let's remember the almonds this time," Julie said, opening the bag.

Ivy pressed an almond onto each cookie, while Mrs. Ling showed Julie how to brush beaten egg white over the top.

"Wait!" Ivy's big brown eyes lit up as she picked up her broken Ghirardelli chocolate bar. "What if we put a little piece of chocolate next to each almond?"

Julie's eyes sparkled. "Mmm, that sounds super yummy!"

"Can we, Mama?" Ivy asked.

"Well, it's not how traditional Chinese almond cookies are, but that's okay," said Ivy's mom. "Why don't I cut up the chocolate into little pieces, and you two can add it to the dough."

When the last tray of cookies was out of the oven, Ivy set a plate of cooled cookies on the table. "These look good," her mother exclaimed. Ivy and Julie held their breath as she took a bite. Mrs. Ling chewed slowly. She took another bite. "Girls, I'm disappointed." Ivy and Julie glanced nervously at each other. "For years I have been known as the best Chinese almond cookie baker in North Beach. But today, I think I have been replaced. These are delicious!" The girls beamed as Mrs. Ling continued.

"This chocolate chunk on top? What a great new twist!"

"That's it!" said Ivy. "In honor of my team, I'm going to name these Chinese Almond Twisters."

Andrew poked his head into the kitchen. "Hey, now *those* look like cookies!" He helped himself to one. "Mmmmm, Mom, these are your best ever. I especially like the chocolate." Andrew turned to his sister. "See, you might as well give up even trying. There's no way you'll ever make cookies as good as these."

Julie, Ivy, and Mrs. Ling burst out laughing.

"What?" Andrew said through a mouthful of cookie. "What did I say?"

IVY'S DILEMMA

On Monday Ivy walked into the Y. She passed the glass cabinet filled with team trophies and photos of the gymnasts, including several of her.

"Good news, girls," Coach Gloria announced. "We made enough money to have pizza at our party!" A cheer went up. The bake sale had been so much fun. Ivy's Chinese Almond Twisters had sold out almost immediately.

That afternoon, Ivy breezed through her floor, vault, and uneven bar exercises. But when it came time for the balance beam, her arms and legs would not cooperate. Easy moves like a 180-degree pivot suddenly became difficult, and Ivy imagined the beam had turned into a circus tightrope with no net below.

If anyone saw me, she thought, *they'd think I was a beginner—and a terrible one. And if I mess up at the tournament again, I won't be helping the team, I'll be hurting it.*

"Coach Gloria," Ivy said, swallowing the lump in her throat, "do you think I can scratch the beam at the tournament?"

Her coach frowned. "Ivy, you scratched last time and only competed in three events. You know I like my girls to compete in the all-around." Ivy studied the chalk on her hands. She couldn't meet her coach's eyes. "I understand your worry," Coach Gloria assured her. "But that's all the more reason you need to try again. Come on, I'll spot you."

"Yes, Coach," Ivy said softly.

The rest of the afternoon, Ivy's stomach was in a knot. Every time she attempted her routine, she slipped off the beam. Nothing was going right. She felt as if her body was betraying her.

That night, when she and her mother arrived home, Ivy was still all wound up with anxiety. As soon as they stepped inside, she could smell the

familiar aroma of garlic and stir-fried noodles.
The takeout cartons were already on the
dining table. Mr. Ling and Andrew were
opening them, and Missy was setting out
the chopsticks.

"Happy Panda again?" Ivy griped. "I'm so tired
of Chinese food."

Her family suddenly grew silent. Ivy turned
around to see Gung Gung and Po Po walking quietly
past the dining room toward the front door. She
covered her mouth, but it was too late—the terrible
words had already been said. How Ivy wished she
could take them back! She waited for someone to
scold her, but no one said a word. Ivy felt her face
burn. She lowered her head so that she wouldn't
have to look at anyone, and ate her meal in silence.

On Saturday morning, while Andrew fought off
imaginary bad guys using sticks as nunchucks, Ivy
trudged through Washington Square Park. All week
she had been dreading going to the Happy Panda
before Chinese school. "Ivy, hurry up," her brother
shouted, "or we'll be late for breakfast!"

Gung Gung and Po Po greeted her warmly. Next to Ivy's bowl of jook was an egg custard tart, one of her favorite treats. Ivy felt ashamed. Even after her awful words, her grandparents were still treating her with kindness. She forced herself to eat every bite of her breakfast, but she could barely say a word. Po Po kept up a cheerful patter and didn't seem to notice.

After Chinese school, Julie was waiting on Ivy's front steps. "Let's go for a walk," she suggested. As they strolled past the Italian restaurants and boutiques that lined the streets of North Beach, Ivy was quiet.

"What's up, Poison Ivy?"

"Nothing."

Julie stopped walking. "I know you, Ivy Ling. Tell me what's wrong."

Ivy was too ashamed to tell Julie about her grandparents. Instead, she blurted out, "I have to do a family history project for Chinese school and I'm behind. My parents are too busy to help me."

That much was true. All week Ivy had asked, "Mama, can you help me with this family tree?"

"When I get some time, Ivy."

"Dad, can you tell me some stories about our relatives?"

"Sure, Ivy, but not right now."

As the girls neared the City Lights Bookstore, they spied a crowd gathering on the corner. In the middle was a young Asian woman waving her arms and frantically shouting in a strange language. Everyone looked concerned, but no one could understand her. As Ivy listened, her heart began to race. The words sounded familiar. The woman was speaking Chinese! She was saying something about a little boy, but what?

Ivy pushed into the crowd. "Please let me through," she shouted. "I can help!"

Ivy spoke haltingly to the young woman in Chinese. The woman's words came fast and frantic through her tears. Ivy nodded and then turned to the crowd. "Her little boy is lost! He's three years old and has short black hair. He's wearing jeans and an orange T-shirt. His name is Sam."

Soon everybody was searching for Sam. His mother clung to Ivy's hand and called out for her son in Chinese. All around people yelled, "Sam! Sam, where are you?"

Suddenly Ivy looked up to see another woman hurrying down the street. Holding her hand was a little boy wearing an orange T-shirt.

"Sam!" his mother shouted, running over and scooping him up in her arms.

Quickly, word got out that Sam had been found. "*Mm goy,*" Sam's mother said to Ivy and the woman.

"She says 'thank you,'" Ivy explained. She turned to Sam's mother. "*Mm sigh hark hay.* You're welcome."

As Ivy and Julie turned to continue their walk, they overheard a man telling his wife, "See that young girl? If it weren't for her, that little boy might still be lost."

Julie nudged Ivy. "You're a hero!"

Ivy felt warm inside. *Wait until Mrs. Chan hears about this!*

That night at the dinner table, Ivy finally had something to say. She told her family about helping Sam's mother find her little boy.

"That's wonderful, Ivy," her mother said.

Her father grinned. "Ivy, fine job."

She looked at Andrew and waited for him to crack a joke, but instead he nodded and said, "Cool."

Ivy took a big bite of her chow mein. It tasted good tonight.

"You'll both have an opportunity to use your Chinese at the annual Ling family reunion," Mr. Ling noted as he piled more bok choy on his plate.

"Will it be at the Happy Panda again?" Andrew asked.

Mrs. Ling nodded. "Yes, and this time it's going to be both sides of our family! Gung Gung and Po Po are really excited about this, and so are we." Her eyes sparkled, and she and Ivy's father smiled at each other.

Ivy was pleased to see her parents looking happy. They had been so busy and tired lately, it sometimes seemed as if they had forgotten how to have a good time. But Ivy wasn't sure how she felt about the Ling family reunion. Sure, she enjoyed the festivities and seeing her cousins, but some of her ancient aunties and uncles were—well, they were weird. They did strange things and told such ridiculous stories, making Ivy squirm with embarrassment.

Great-Uncle Henry was always yelling, "Henry Fong, come on down!" as he reenacted the time he won his color television on *The Price Is Right*. Auntie Lu loved reminding everyone that when she was an acrobat back in China, she juggled teacups. If anyone showed even the slightest bit of interest, she'd demonstrate. This amused the little cousins, but Ivy and the older kids would slink away, giggling at their odd auntie.

Then there was Andrew, Andrew, Andrew.

"Andrew, look how big and strong you are!"

"Andrew, straight A's again?"

"Andrew, I heard you won another kung fu tournament!"

All the relatives fussing and fawning over Andrew drove Ivy crazy. So what if he was the eldest boy cousin? Big deal. Besides, who cared what the crazy old relatives thought, anyway? Still, Ivy couldn't help thinking, *Maybe if I do really well at my tournament, they'll notice* me, *too.*

At gymnastics practice after school, Ivy worked extra hard on the balance beam. She didn't even mind when Coach Gloria yelled out, "Higher, Ivy," and "Do that pivot over," and "Relax, Ivy, relax!" Ivy knew that her coach was only trying to get her to do her best. And she was improving—she could feel it.

Her balance was steady and her footing was solid. She leaped high in the air and landed with poise. As she did a back walkover, Ivy imagined adding another trophy to the fireplace mantel.

"Great dismount!" Coach Gloria called out.

Ivy grinned. Now, if only she could repeat it in competition. It was one thing to do well at the Y, but she knew from experience that it was entirely different with judges scrutinizing her every move.

After gymnastics Ivy walked with her mother and Missy through Chinatown. Ivy was glowing—it was the best balance beam practice she'd had since her fall. Just thinking about the tournament on Saturday and the pizza party afterward made Ivy feel like skipping. But as they neared the Happy Panda, her bubbly mood fizzled and her steps grew slower.

"Ivy, why are you straggling?" Her mother's voice was impatient.

"You go ahead." Ivy pretended to be interested in a window display of dragons. "I want to look at some things in Mrs. Quan's store."

Her mother sighed. "Okay, I'll meet you in front of the restaurant."

Ivy waited until Missy and her mother were inside. Then she peeked through the window in time to see them hug Po Po and Gung Gung. Once more, shame washed over her. She slipped her hands into her pockets and turned away.

That night, as the family gathered around the dining room table, Mrs. Ling served dinner from the familiar takeout cartons. Ivy looked at the *gailan* on her plate. Gailan was the Chinese version of broccoli, something she didn't like no matter what country it was from. The other stuff was okay, like the spicy shrimp and the fried rice.

"I finished my paper on Bruce Lee," Andrew announced.

Ivy picked up a single grain of rice with her chopsticks and examined it. She hadn't even started her family history project.

"So," Mr. Ling said, fishing a tea leaf out of his cup. "Great-Uncle Henry and Great-Auntie Winnie got their bus tickets for Saturday."

"What for?" Ivy asked. Had her parents told them about her gymnastics tournament? Were they coming to watch her compete?

Her father laughed. "What for? For the family reunion, what else?"

"Saturday?" Ivy stammered. "It's this Saturday?"

"Why, yes, Ivy, you knew that," said Mr. Ling.

Ivy shook her head. "No, no," she cried. "I didn't, honestly. This Saturday is the all-city gymnastics tournament. I'm competing with the Twisters!"

"Well," Mr. Ling said, pausing to take a sip of tea, "you'll just have to miss the tournament."

Mrs. Ling finished wiping Missy's face. "Ivy has been practicing all year for this meet. It's very important to her."

"This reunion is important to our families," Mr. Ling replied. "Ah Yeh and Ah Mah are flying in from New York. Po Po's been planning the menu for weeks."

Ivy's mother nodded. "I know. But Ivy's team is counting on her."

"All of the relatives are expecting our entire family," Mr. Ling declared.

Ivy, Andrew, and Missy were quiet as their parents argued back and forth. Ivy's throat tightened and she wished she could just disappear. Finally, her mother looked at her. "Perhaps the final decision should be left up to Ivy."

"Yes," her father agreed. "Ivy, you decide between the tournament and the family reunion."

"Give it some thought," her mother said tenderly. "When you've made your choice, let us know."

Ivy swallowed. It would be so much easier if her parents would just tell her what to do.

On Tuesday after school, when Ivy got to the YWCA, the other girls were stretching and talking. Quickly, Ivy changed into her red-and-gold leotard and joined them.

"The all-city meet is in just four more days!" said Jennifer. "Aren't you excited?"

"Yes," Ivy said. She was—but she couldn't bring herself to tell her teammate that she might not be able to go.

That afternoon, everything seemed to come together. Ivy's tumbling passes went off with ease. She got good height in her vaults. On the uneven bars, her timing was perfect. And on the balance beam, Ivy completed her routine without making a single error. All her hard work was paying off.

Maybe I should go to the tournament, Ivy thought

as she ran through her beam routine one last time. *The team needs me, and I'm definitely improving. Plus there's the big pizza party afterward.*

Just then she saw two familiar figures walk into the gym. Ivy gasped and nearly lost her balance. What were Po Po and Gung Gung doing here?

She dismounted and approached her grandparents nervously. "She's a real asset to the Twisters," Coach Gloria was telling them, as her grandparents glowed with pride.

"Ah! There you are," Gung Gung exclaimed. "Ivy, you're coming with us." He paused when he saw the worried look on her face. "It's okay, your mother gave us permission."

Permission for what? Ivy wondered nervously. But instead of asking, Ivy silently gathered her belongings. Was she in trouble?

Ivy clutched her gym bag to her chest and followed her grandparents as they left the Y. She longed to beg them for forgiveness, but the words caught in her throat.

At last she could no longer keep her feelings in. Small sobs began to escape, followed by bigger and bigger ones.

Po Po stopped and turned around. "Why the tears?" she said softly.

"I'm soooooo sorry," Ivy sobbed.

"Sorry for what?" Gung Gung asked.

"For saying I was sick of Chinese food." Ivy gulped for air. "It was terrible of me."

Po Po took Ivy's hands in hers. "You were speaking your feelings. That's no crime in America."

"Ivy, you're our number one granddaughter, and we love you," Gung Gung assured her. "Now, stop blubbering. We have someplace special to go!"

Ivy hugged her grandparents. As they continued down the street and then stopped to wait for a cable car, she felt as light as a feather.

"Where are we going?" Ivy asked as the cable car conductor took their money. Instead of answering, Po Po just smiled mysteriously.

"This is our stop," Gung Gung finally said.

After walking a couple of blocks, they slowed. Her grandfather's eyes twinkled mischievously as he held open a door. "Frankie's Diner," he said matter-of-factly.

"We love Frankie's," whispered Po Po. "Thirty years—no changes!"

46

Ivy was still confused as she slid into a red vinyl booth.

"You know, we get tired of Chinese food all the time, too," Gung Gung confided.

"Sometime I think, 'Oh my, I see another bowl of rice, I faint!'" Po Po laughed. "So every now and then, we treat ourselves to a night out."

"But we can't have our customers see us eating at someone else's restaurant," Gung Gung explained. "So we have to go far away. Some nights we eat Italian food, other times Greek. Tonight, good old American hamburgers!"

Ivy didn't even have to look at the menu. "A cheeseburger, fries, and a chocolate shake," she told the waitress.

"Make that two," said Gung Gung.

"Make that three," Po Po echoed.

Talk soon turned to the reunion. "This year everyone is coming," Gung Gung said.

"Yes, yes," said Po Po excitedly. "I'm planning extra special Chinese feast. Ivy, you will be most impressed!"

"We bought fancy paper lanterns," Gung Gung added. "After the reunion, you can have one for your room."

Ivy smiled. Her grandparents' excitement was infectious. *Maybe I should choose the reunion,* Ivy mused. *It would mean so much to my family.* Just then, the waitress appeared with their food.

"Cheeseburgers!" Gung Gung declared, clapping his hands. "Now, Ivy, remember—no one can know we don't eat Chinese food every day. This is our secret," he said, winking. "Promise you won't tell!"

"I promise!" Ivy winked back. She lifted up her milk shake. "Here's to the family reunion, and to Chinese food, and to cheeseburgers—every now and then."

DRAGONS RULE

 "Are you absolutely sure?" Mrs. Ling looked closely at Ivy. "I know how important gymnastics is to you."

Ivy's father put on his security guard jacket. "You're not trying to get her to change her mind, are you?"

"No, I just want to make sure Ivy has really thought this through."

"I have," Ivy said, hoping her voice wouldn't waver. "At dinner with Gung Gung and Po Po, I realized how important this was to the family."

"Wonderful!" Mr. Ling smiled broadly. "Everyone will be thrilled to see you at the reunion."

Ivy smiled back as she watched her father leave.

After he was gone, she stood staring out the front door.

"Honey, are you okay?" her mother asked.

Ivy nodded. "It's just that it's going to be really hard to tell Coach Gloria."

"Would you like me to talk to her?"

"No, that's okay." Ivy took a deep breath. "I'll do it."

The next day, school flew by and before Ivy knew it, it was time for gymnastics. But instead of hurrying to the YWCA as usual, Ivy took her time. She stopped twice to tighten her shoelaces and then lingered at the Lucky Five and Dime. On one of the posters Bruce Lee was flying high through the air in a kick position. His form and precision were impressive. Ivy could see why Andrew admired him so much.

Bruce Lee would have been a wonderful gymnast, Ivy mused. *I wonder which he would have picked—the family reunion or the tournament?*

"You're here!" Coach Gloria called out when Ivy finally appeared. "I was afraid you weren't going to show up."

"Um, can I talk to you for a moment?" Ivy stammered.

"Of course. What is it?" When Ivy hesitated, her coach said, "It's about the tournament, isn't it?"

"Yes." Ivy took a deep breath and forced herself to speak. "It's just that I don't think I can—"

"Ivy," Coach Gloria said gently, "I know what you're going to say. Don't worry—it'll be okay."

"Are you sure?" Ivy asked, confused. Her mother must have already told Coach Gloria about the reunion.

"Yes," her coach reassured her. "It's perfectly natural to worry, but I promise you'll be fine." She gave Ivy a little hug. "I've seen how hard you've been working. You're looking really strong on the balance beam, and I know you'll come through. The team is counting on you."

Ivy opened her mouth but only a small squeak came out. She cleared her throat and tried again. "But—well . . . " Coach Gloria smiled encouragingly. "Um . . . I should probably get to practice."

Coach Gloria patted her on the back. "That's the spirit, Ivy!"

❧

That night at dinner, Ivy was silent. She couldn't even lift her eyes off her lap.

"What's *your* problem?" Andrew asked. "Aren't you even going to complain about the Chinese food?"

"Ivy?" Her mother sounded concerned. "Is everything all right?"

"I know what this is about," Andrew said. Ivy gave him a sideways glance. "It's because you haven't even started your family history project, have you?"

Ivy shook her head.

"Oh, Ivy," her father said, putting down his chopsticks. "I am so sorry. I promised to tell you about your relatives, and I keep forgetting. Is that what's bothering you?"

Ivy shook her head. Her eyes filled with tears. She blinked them back and blurted out, "I couldn't tell Coach Gloria about the reunion. She thinks I'm going to the tournament."

"What?" Mr. Ling asked, surprised.

Ivy pushed her chair away from the table and ran to her room. As she sobbed into her pillow, she could hear her parents' voices rising.

"She said she was going to the reunion," her father said.

"Her gymnastics team is counting on her," her mother insisted. "Ivy's worked very hard for this."

"If people are making the effort to come hundreds of miles, my daughter can certainly miss one meet."

"This isn't just any meet, it's the all-city tournament . . ."

Suddenly Ivy wished she had never started gymnastics. Then her parents wouldn't be arguing now. It was all her fault. Was this what it was like at Julie's house before her parents got a divorce?

After a while the voices lowered to a soft murmur. Then there was a knock on her door. "Honey? May we come in?" her mother asked.

"Yes, Mama," Ivy said, wiping her tears on her sleeve.

No one was arguing anymore, but still the air felt thick.

"I didn't realize how much this tournament means to you," Mr. Ling said solemnly. "Ivy, if this is so important to you, then I will respect that."

Ivy looked up and met her father's eyes. They

looked kind, not angry. "Are you sure?"

"I'm sure."

"Thank you, Daddy," she cried, flying into his arms.

Mr. Ling caught Ivy and hugged her back. "Thank your mother," he laughed. "She's going to make a fine lawyer."

"Mama, I'll do my best—I'll make you proud of me," Ivy promised.

"Honey," her mother said, "we're already proud of you."

On Thursday morning, Ivy poured milk over her Lucky Charms. She watched the marshmallow bits swim around and then plunged her spoon into the cereal. *Two days, only two days, until the all-city tournament.* There would be hundreds of competitors—the very best gymnasts in San Francisco.

"Try to bring home some trophies," Andrew said before chugging a tall glass of milk.

Ivy's stomach did a flip worthy of a 9.9 on the judges' scale. She glared at her brother. "Easy for you to say! I'm not like you."

Andrew wiped off his milk mustache. "What's that supposed to mean?"

"You're lucky. You get good grades, you're good at kung fu, and everybody loves you, even teachers," Ivy said, her voice rising. "You have all the luck."

"Hey, I work hard for my grades—and for my kung fu trophies. So did Little Dragon," Andrew said, pointing to the image of Bruce Lee on his T-shirt. "So don't tell me that it's all just luck. We dragons *make* our luck. Dragons rule!"

Ivy groaned. Great. Now her brother thought he was a dragon. "Geez, Andrew. Forget I even said anything!"

Yet that afternoon as Ivy went through her gymnastics routines, she could not forget Andrew's words. *We dragons make our luck.* Was there some truth to that? Ivy let out a small sigh. To even think that she could be like a dragon, or like Andrew or Bruce Lee, was silly. They were fearless. She was not.

After practice, Ivy sat in the kitchen of the Happy Panda watching the waiters and cooks. They worked like well-choreographed gymnasts—turning, balancing plates, and never missing a beat.

"Ivy, come here," Po Po called out.

abacus

In the cramped little office off the back of the restaurant, an abacus sat on the desk alongside an adding machine. Old black-and-white photos lined the walls. Ivy ran her fingers across a picture of her mother when she was about Ivy's age. She looked so self-assured, like Andrew.

Gung Gung set down a plate of sliced oranges in front of Ivy. "Tell us what's bothering you," Po Po said.

"You can tell something's wrong?"

Po Po chuckled softly. "Ivy, I can see in your heart, always."

Ivy sighed. "No matter how well I do in practice, I'm still afraid I'll fall off the balance beam."

"Hmmm, that would be awful," her grandfather mused. "If you fall, the world will end."

"Well, noooo," Ivy said.

"Oh! That's right, if you fall, you will turn into a bitter melon, roll down the street, and get run over by a trolley car."

"Oh, you shush," Po Po said to Gung Gung. She turned back to Ivy. Her sparkling brown eyes grew serious. "In school long ago, teacher ask me to give speech about America. My English," she said,

56

shaking her head, "not good. I scared everybody laugh. But still, I want to tell how I love my new country. Then I think, I not giving speech to impress others about me, but because I have important thing to say. I decide, I will say what is in my heart."

"What happened?" Ivy asked.

"I focus on my words, my feelings, not audience."

"And you weren't scared?"

"I was scared," Po Po admitted, "but I believed in my speech, and that gave me courage."

"She got a standing ovation," Gung Gung added proudly.

Po Po blushed. She leaned toward Ivy and confided, "A nice boy help me with my English when I practice." She and Gung Gung shared a smile.

"She was the prettiest girl in Chinatown—and still is," said Gung Gung, giving Ivy a wink.

"Shush!" Po Po said, playfully brushing him away. She turned back to Ivy. "It's okay to be scared, but enjoy your tournament. Gymnastics is in your heart. I can see that."

THE BIG DAY

On Saturday morning Ivy woke up early and slipped on her warm-up suit over her Twisters leotard. She pulled her hair back into a sleek ponytail and reached for a red ribbon. As she stepped out of her room, she could feel the buzz of excitement running through the Ling household.

"Do you need any help, Mama?" Ivy asked, handing her mom the ribbon. Mrs. Ling and Missy were already busy making colorful flower decorations out of tissue paper and pipe cleaners.

"No thanks, honey," her mother said, tying the ribbon around Ivy's ponytail. "We're fine."

After breakfast, Ivy wandered into the dining room. Andrew was writing name cards for the tables.

"Would you like me to do some name cards?" Ivy offered.

"Nope. I'm almost done. Don't these look great?"

Ivy nodded. They did look great. Next to each name, Andrew had drawn a small dragon.

"Do you need me to do anything?" Ivy asked her father. He was going over the guest list.

"Thanks," he said, "but everything is all ready."

Ivy peered over his shoulder at the list and winced. Her name had been crossed off. Ivy felt a small ache in her heart.

Just then, the doorbell rang. Ivy opened the door.

"Are you ready for the tournament, Ivy?" asked Julie. "My dad's waiting in the car."

"Let me just get my stuff." Ivy hurried to her room and grabbed her gym bag.

"Good luck, Ivy," her mother whispered as she gave her a hug.

"Do your best!" her father called out from the living room.

Missy put a red paper flower and something soft and cuddly in Ivy's hands. "These are for you."

Ivy took the flower and looked at her sister's

precious stuffed lion. "Oh, Missy! I can't take Roary. He's yours."

"You can borrow him. He brings me good luck."

Ivy ruffled Missy's hair. "Thank you."

Just as Ivy was getting into Mr. Albright's car, Andrew appeared. "Here." He handed her an envelope. "Don't open it until you get to the tournament." Before Ivy could say anything, Andrew was gone.

The college sports arena was bigger than any gym Ivy had ever seen before. Excitement, fear, and joy hit her at the same time. Ivy's eyes opened wide as she tried to take in the whole scene. Hundreds of gymnasts covered the competition floor. Judges greeted each other. Fans filled the bleachers. Some held up posters cheering on their teams. Julie gave Ivy a quick hug, and then she and her father climbed into the bleachers while Ivy searched for the Twisters. She saw gymnasts milling around in sleek leotards and warm-up outfits in every color, but no red and gold.

I'll never find my team! Ivy thought as she looked

frantically around the huge arena.

"Ivy!" she heard Coach Gloria call out. "Over here."

Ivy turned around and waved excitedly. "Here I come, Coach!"

After warm-ups, Ivy's first event was her favorite—the floor. Ivy took her position. When she heard the first bars of her music over the P.A. system, she smiled and began her tumbling pass. As Ivy did a round-off, a back handspring, and then a back flip, she felt as if she were dancing on clouds. Her body lifted itself effortlessly as she flew across the mat. It seemed as if she had just begun when she heard the final notes of her music.

Ivy couldn't stop grinning as she saluted the judges. She held her breath as her scores were tallied. When her marks were posted, a cheer went up. Ivy was in the lead! She wouldn't know how she had placed until everyone had competed on floor, but no matter what, she knew she had done her best.

Next up was the vault. Ivy had always done fairly well at this, although she could never seem to get quite enough height. When her turn came, Ivy took a deep breath and signaled that she was ready. Running as fast as she could, she built up speed, leaped onto the springboard, and launched herself into the air. She pushed off the horse with her arms and stuck her landing. A nice, clean vault.

Ivy paced with her hands on her hips as she waited for her score. Apparently the judges were as pleased with her vault as she was, and they gave her high marks. Her second vault wasn't nearly as good, but Ivy was happy just to get the event out of the way.

The other Twisters were doing well too, and several had scored personal bests. "Keep this up, girls," Coach Gloria told them. "Remember, our combined scores determine team rankings."

By the time it was Ivy's turn for the uneven bars, lunch had already passed. She had been too nervous to eat anything, but Coach Gloria had forced her to have some apple slices dipped in peanut butter.

On the unevens, her routine flowed smoothly. Now there was only one event left—the balance beam.

Ivy paced nervously, trying not to think about what had happened the last time she had competed on the beam. Suddenly she remembered something. She reached inside her gym bag and gave Roary a squeeze. Just thinking of

Missy's sweet, earnest face when she'd handed
Roary over that morning pushed the other thoughts
out of her mind.

Then Ivy opened Andrew's envelope.
Smiling at her in a Polaroid photograph were her parents, Missy, and
Andrew. In the center, Andrew was
holding up a big poster. On it he had
painted a beautiful dragon saying,
"Good luck, Ivy!"

Ivy could hardly believe it.
Andrew had made this just for her. He
had painted the dragon and gotten the family
together—not an easy task with their parents'
schedules—so that he could make this special
photograph for her. To give her good luck.

"Come on, Ivy, you're up next!" Coach Gloria
shouted.

Ivy pressed the photo to her heart before tucking
it back into her gym bag. She looked up and saw
Julie, who was standing and waving in the audience.
Ivy gave her a small nod.

As Ivy approached the balance beam, she tried to
focus. This wasn't about the hundreds of people in

the audience, she told herself sternly. It wasn't about the forty competitors in her division, or even the two judges staring at her. It was just Ivy and the balance beam. For the next ninety seconds, nothing else mattered.

Ivy mounted and began moving gracefully across the beam. She landed her leaps solidly. When she wobbled on her pivot, she slowed and steadied herself. She even remembered to smile. Before Ivy knew it, she was nearing the end of her routine. Could she finish without falling? Ivy's breath tightened as she swung her arms up to begin the back walkover. She fought down a rush of panic as she arched backward and reached for the beam. She could feel beads of sweat breaking out on her forehead. What if her palms were sweaty and slippery? Then she heard Po Po's gentle voice telling her, "Gymnastics is in your heart."

Ivy had practiced this move hundreds of times. Her body knew what to do, she reminded herself. *Dragons make their luck.* She focused and felt a surge of energy flow through her as her hands gripped the beam. She kicked one leg over, then the other, planting each foot firmly on the beam, and stood up gracefully as the audience applauded. Brimming with confidence, Ivy went into her dismount. She flew high in the air and nailed her landing.

Coach Gloria gave her a gigantic hug. "You did it, Ivy! And you looked like you were having fun up there. You looked so confident!"

Ivy's face flushed. "I had help from a dragon," she explained.

Her coach laughed. "I'm not sure what that means, but it certainly seemed to work for you!"

At last it was time for the awards ceremony. Ivy earned a fourth-place medal in the vault—and a third-place on the beam! And when she heard the announcer say, "The first-place trophy on the floor exercise goes to Ivy Ling of the Twisters," her heart soared. She held the trophy up high so that Julie could see it.

After the individual trophies were given out, the Twisters all held hands nervously.

"The second-place all-city team trophy goes to . . . the Twisters gymnastics team!" said the announcer, and Ivy and her teammates began screaming and jumping up and down.

The girls took turns holding the giant trophy

while their parents took pictures. Ivy stood on the sidelines watching. She was the only one without her family with her. As she reached into her bag to look at Andrew's photo again, Missy's tissue paper flower fell to the ground. Ivy picked it up and cradled it in her hand. She wondered what was happening at the reunion. Was it even still going on?

Ivy gazed at Andrew's photo. She had missed a lot of the reunion, but maybe she didn't have to miss all of it. *Dragons make their luck.* How she spent the rest of the day was up to her.

Ivy tapped Coach Gloria on the shoulder. "Coach," Ivy said, presenting the flower to her, "I know we're having the pizza party, but I won't be able to attend. There's somewhere else I need to be."

❀

"First stop," Mr. Albright announced as he pulled the car up in front of Ivy's house.

"I'll be right back," Ivy promised. Julie and her father waited as she rushed inside. Ivy looked behind her bedroom door and smiled. There was her lucky Chinese dress, waiting for her.

❀

66

Loud laughter and chatter in both English and Chinese spilled out of the Happy Panda banquet room. Ivy smoothed the front of her red silk dress, linked arms with Julie, and then entered. Mr. Albright followed, carrying Ivy's first-place trophy, her medals, and Roary.

Andrew leaped onto a chair and shouted, "Hey, everyone—Ivy's here!"

A cheer went up. Ivy felt like a celebrity.

As Mr. Albright handed Ivy her trophy, Missy cried, "Look! Ivy won!" A second cheer filled the room, and Ivy blushed nearly as red as her dress.

Ah Yeh and Ah Mah, her father's parents, came rushing up to embrace her, followed by her mother and father.

"Tell us all about the tournament, Ivy," said her mother.

"Time for that later!" Po Po cried. "First, great gymnast and guests must eat!"

"Oh, no, that's not necessary," said Mr. Albright, handing Roary to Missy. "We're just dropping Ivy off."

"Of course it's necessary," Gung Gung insisted. "You and Julie are like family, too!"

A cheer went up. Ivy felt like a celebrity.

"Sit. Eat!" Po Po ordered. She signaled the waiters. Instantly, plates of steaming hot food appeared, including Ivy's favorites—barbecued duck and sweet and sour pork.

"Mmm, this looks delicious," said Mr. Albright as Po Po filled his plate. "Ivy, you are so lucky your grandparents own a Chinese restaurant."

"I know," she said, winking at Po Po.

"I've never had so much to eat in my life," Julie whispered as they ate. "Your grandparents are stuffing me with food!"

"It's what they do," Ivy laughed. "It means they like you!"

Later, as Ivy greeted her dozens of cousins, aunts, uncles, and other assorted relations, everyone admired her first-place trophy and her medals. After a while the trophy grew heavy, so Ivy set it down. Even without the trophy, everyone seemed very pleased to see her.

Great-Uncle Henry was talking to Missy. *Probably telling her about the color TV he won*, Ivy figured. Her poor sister must be trapped. But Missy looked rapt with attention.

"—and so, I could stay in China," Great-Uncle

Henry was saying. "Or I could journey to the Gold Mountain."

Missy's jaw dropped. "Was it made of real gold?"

"No," Great-Uncle Henry explained. "That's what we called California in the old days." Missy looked disappointed. "My plan was to make my fortune here and then return to Canton a rich man."

Ivy sat down beside Missy. "Were you scared to leave China?"

"Of course I was! I wasn't much older than Andrew. But I didn't let that stop me. America is the land of opportunity and freedom—and free televisions!"

"Wait," Ivy exclaimed. "This is perfect for my family history project." She bolted from the table and returned with a notebook.

"I worked in a sewing factory," Auntie Verna recalled. "We worked twelve hours a day, six days a week."

"My father was once a letter writer," said Uncle Wan. "People who couldn't read or write paid him to send letters back home to China for them."

"Your great-great-grandfather worked on the railroads," Ah Mah said proudly. "It was thanks to men like him that the West was settled."

At last, Ivy closed her notebook. Amazing stories overflowed from its pages—enough to write a dozen family history reports. She turned to Auntie Lu. "Did you like being an acrobat when you were in China?"

"Yes," she murmured, fingering her strands of pearls. "Maybe you get gymnastics skills from me!" Auntie Lu hesitated, and then asked, "I don't suppose you'd like to see me perform?"

"I'd love to," said Ivy.

Beaming, Auntie Lu stood up. She tapped a serving spoon against a water glass, and when she had everyone's attention, she held an empty plate high above her head. Silence swept across the room.

All eyes were on Auntie Lu. With grand flowing gestures, she picked up a chopstick and balanced the plate on top of it. As she spun the plate and raised it in the air, everyone applauded.

Julie came up to Ivy. "These are from your grandmother," she said, handing her a plate of Chinese Almond Twisters. "She says your mom gave her the recipe."

As the girls munched on cookies, Ivy looked

around the Happy Panda. To Missy's delight,
Auntie Lu was now juggling two teacups, a soup
ladle—and Roary. Great-Uncle Henry was reenacting
the time he won a TV on *The Price Is Right* for Julie's
father, who laughed and laughed when Uncle Henry
shouted, "Henry Fong, come on down!" Andrew
was pretending to be a dragon and chasing his little
cousins. He ran past Ivy and helped himself to a
Chinese Almond Twister. "Thanks, Sis," he yelled.
"Dragons rule!"

"Dragons rule!" she shouted back.

In a quiet corner, Ivy spied her parents. Her
mother and father sat close together, gazing happily
around the room.

"Gosh, Ivy," Julie said wistfully. "It must be nice
to be part of a big family like this."

Ivy broke into a big smile. "It's wonderful," she
said. "I had no idea how lucky I was!"

LOOKING BACK

CHINESE AMERICANS

Author Lisa Yee's family. Her mother, Marylin Yee, is the little girl on the right, leaning against her father's knee.

Although Ivy's family is Chinese American, Ivy herself feels 100 percent American. Like many Chinese Americans, she was born in America, and her parents were, too. But her grandmother Po Po and some of her other relatives were born in China. When they moved to America, they brought some of their Chinese customs with them.

The Chinese first began coming to California during

the 1849 gold rush. Young men left behind poverty and war in China to seek their fortune in the "Gold Mountain." Although very few Chinese got rich mining gold, they found other ways to earn a

Canton, China, in the mid-1800s

living, often by farming, fishing, and doing laundry. When the gold rush was over, many settled in the San Francisco neighborhood that became known as Chinatown.

Chinese men in a mining camp

A decade later, in the 1860s, the Central Pacific Railroad needed workers to lay train tracks through the Sierra Nevada mountains—a hard and dangerous job. The railroad managers found that the Chinese were brave and hardworking, so they brought over more laborers from China to help build the *transcontinental* railroad, which went all the way across America.

These early Chinese workers were all men. They did not intend to *immigrate*, or live in the United States for the rest of their lives. Instead, they hoped to make money for a few years and then return as wealthy men to their families in China. But most of them never made it back. They ended up settling in San Francisco, Los Angeles, New York, and other cities.

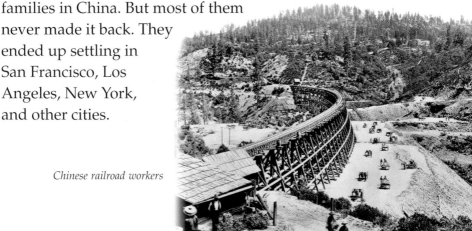
Chinese railroad workers

The "Chinatown" neighborhoods in these cities were like little islands of China in America. People spoke Chinese on the street and in shops and restaurants. They could worship at Chinese temples, observe Chinese holidays, and be treated by doctors who practiced Chinese medicine. Even the newspapers and street signs were in Chinese.

For the Chinese men, life in America was somewhat better than the poverty in China, but their lives were not easy. They were not allowed to own land or to bring their families over from China. The men had a hard time finding jobs, and they faced prejudice, discrimination, and even violence. They were forbidden by law from becoming American citizens unless they had been born in America.

This ad tells readers that if they buy a washing machine (a new invention) and do their own laundry, they'll help put the Chinese out of business. Many prejudiced people wanted the Chinese to go back to China.

City Hall after the earthquake. At right, a Chinese man gazes at the destruction.

Then, in 1906, an enormous earthquake rocked San Francisco, followed by raging fires. The quake caused terrible damage and suffering, but it helped the Chinese in an unexpected way, by destroying the building that held the city's birth records. Seizing their chance, many Chinese Californians claimed to be native-born. Since there were no records to check, their claims could not be easily denied. Now, at last, they could bring over their wives and children. Some couples had lived apart for 10 or 20 years!

In 1965, an new law permitted many more Chinese to

Chinese immigrants came off the ship at Angel Island, in the San Francisco Bay, where they waited to be processed.

New York City's Chinatown, 1976

immigrate to the United States. By Ivy's time, Chinese immigrants and their descendents lived in cities throughout the United States, and many had become highly successful in their fields. Ivy might have seen TV news stories by a young Chinese American reporter named Connie Chung. Her brother Andrew, like millions of American boys of all races, admired martial artist and movie star Bruce Lee.

Bruce Lee was born in San Francisco but grew up in Hong Kong, where he learned the martial art of kung fu. He returned to the U.S. in his late teens and soon began teaching and refining his own style of kung fu. He acted in a few TV series and made special appearances at martial arts tournaments. By the early 1970s,

Olympic skater Michelle Kwan

In 1981, a young architecture student named Maya Lin won a contest to design the Vietnam War Memorial in Washington, D.C.

Best-selling novelist Amy Tan writes about Chinese American families.

when he was starring in the movie *Enter the Dragon*, he was the biggest martial arts star and the most famous Chinese American—in both China *and* America!

Bruce Lee

Today, there are more than three million Chinese Americans, and thousands of Chinese still immigrate to the United States each year. Chinese restaurants, once found only in big cities, are now extremely popular throughout the United States, and kung fu is taught nearly everywhere in the country. Many Chinese American children attend Chinese school, just like Ivy and Andrew, to stay connected to their heritage. Whether they are recent immigrants or have lived in the U.S. for generations, Chinese Americans continue to share their talents and traditions, enriching all Americans in the process.

*Author Lisa Yee, age 15, at far left, next to her
mother, cousins, and aunts in 1975*

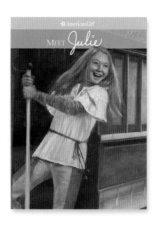

A SNEAK PEEK AT

MEET

Julie

Julie Albright doesn't want to move. Moving means leaving her best friend, Ivy, and her pet rabbit, Nutmeg. Worst of all, it means leaving Dad, now that her parents are divorced.

The world spun—first upside down, then right-side up again—as Julie Albright and her best friend, Ivy Ling, turned cartwheels around the backyard.

"Watch me do a backflip!" called Ivy. She leaned back, stretching her neck like a tree bending in the wind. Soon her shiny black ponytail bounced upside down as she twirled through the air, landing perfectly on two feet.

"I always fall flat on my face!" said Julie. "I'll never be as good as you, no matter how hard I practice." She sighed. "I'm sure going to miss doing gymnastics with you after school every day. What are you going to miss most?"

"Walking to school together and sitting behind you in class," said Ivy. "Passing notes and braiding your hair when the teacher's not looking." Julie had long, straight blond hair, and Ivy could make a teeny tiny braid down one side in seconds.

"Who am I going to be lunch buddies with?" said Julie. "You're the only friend in the world who would trade me your Twinkie for a pickle!"

"Julie!" Mom called from the back porch. "Time

to get a move on. The van will be here in an hour."

Julie and Ivy turned cartwheels all the way to the back steps. "I guess I better get going," said Ivy.

"Not yet!" said Julie. "Come up to my room with me while I make sure I'm all packed."

Upstairs, Julie scooped up Nutmeg, her pet rabbit, from her favorite spot in the laundry basket and plopped down cross-legged next to Ivy on the bed. Ivy stroked Nutmeg's velvet-brown fur, while Julie scratched her pet behind her floppy lop ears. Nutmeg snuffled softly, and her sleepy eyes started to close. "I'm sure gonna miss you, girl," said Julie, kissing her on her wiggly nose. "But Ivy's going to take extra-special good care of you whenever Dad's gone."

The room turned middle-of-the-night quiet. Julie and Ivy couldn't look at each other.

"I still can't believe you're moving," said Ivy, flashing her dark eyes at Julie.

"It's only a few miles away, across town," said Julie. "It's not like I'm moving to Mars."

"I won't be able to blink lights at you from across the street anymore to say good night," said Ivy.

"But we can call each other up," Julie pointed out. "And you'll still see me on the weekends when I come visit my dad." There was that lump again. She felt it every time she thought of being without Dad. She thought she'd gotten used to the idea of her parents being divorced, but now that she wouldn't be living with Dad anymore, suddenly it wasn't just an idea. It was real.

"Here," said Julie. "I made us friendship bracelets. We can both wear them, and think of each other." She handed a colorful knotted bracelet to Ivy.

"Neat!" said Ivy. "And it's red and purple, my favorite colors."

"Red and purple are my favorites, too," said Julie. "Also blue, green, pink, and sometimes yellow!"

"Put it on my ankle," said Ivy, holding out her foot. "Hey, do you have a Magic Marker?"

"What for?" asked Julie, taking out a pen from her box of desk stuff.

"Give me your foot," said Ivy.

Julie held out her once-clean high-top sneaker. She had doodled all over it with markers. Ivy wrote something on the rubber tip of the toe. Julie peered at the letters: A. F. A.

"A Friend Always!" said Julie.

Julie's big sister, Tracy, poked her head into Julie's room. "Mom says to start bringing our stuff down. Set it in the front room."

"Not yet!" Julie protested. "Just a few more minutes." It was bad enough they were making her move. Now they were taking away her last moments with her best friend, too.

"Mom says *now*," said Tracy, sounding annoyed.

Julie got up and tried lifting a too-heavy box, then set it back down and began dragging a garbage bag across the floor instead. "Now I know why they call it Labor Day," she grumbled.

"I guess I better go, for real this time," said Ivy. Julie nodded. The two friends hooked pinkies in a secret handshake they'd had since kindergarten. Neither girl wanted to be the one to let go first.